J
574.52636
PECHTER

WITHDRAWN

What's
in the Deep?

What's in the Deep?

An underwater adventure for children

**Story and photographs
by Alese and Morton Pechter**

ACROPOLIS BOOKS LTD.
WASHINGTON, D.C.

Thank You. . . .

Thank yous can sound like a rambling list but very few projects ever get completed without the help and encouragement of many along the way. Our supporters have given us the tenacity to keep on plugging and we are anxious to acknowledge them publically.

First and foremost to our longtime friend, Jean Michel Cousteau who was the unknowing impetus for our journey to the underwater world; to the sweet, warm "Siren of SCUBA, her Royal Deepness," Sylvia Earle who graciously wrote the beautiful foreword; to Michael Collins, our astronaut friend, the command module pilot for the first landing on the moon, for making us realize so much more how special our underwater world really is; to Phil and Sandy Trupp, who consistently buoyed the spirits and pointed us in the right direction; to Dr. & Mrs. F.G. Walton Smith and Jean Bradfisch for their encouragement at the very beginning; to Jerry & Idaz Greenberg whose expertise and advice always guide us; to Marian Rivman, a gem of a lady who sparkles with insight, imagination, love and creativity, and who is a constant source of inspiration; to Bob and Shirle Gray, the "heart" of DEMA who make us feel proud to be a part of the SCUBA world; to Betsy and Allan Edmund who have always been so generous in their support and help; to the late Gilbert Voss who shared his knowledge about fish behavior with us so that our facts would be correct; to Pam Stacey whose expertise on writing for children was invaluable; to Al and John Hackl, the dynamic guiding lights of Acropolis, for having confidence in our project; to our fabulous editor and publisher, Kathleen Hughes who steers us with love and warmth; to Kathy Cunningham for her astute, artistic eye; to Alan Mirken who was the first book publisher to tell us our project had merit and sent us off to see the "right people;" to Steve Blount who kept us going; to our nephew Aaron Rothschild who first intoned the title; to the Colucci Family who joyfully posed for our photos; to Bertha Pechter; to our fathers, William Pechter and "Doc" Joseph Cohen; to our children, Jay, Todd, Richard, Robin, Stuart and Madeline, and our grandchildren Nelson, Patricia, Joseph, William, Diana and Wyatt for the never-ending love and joy they give to us; and above all to our mother, Norma Newman Cohen who always gave us "vitamins for the soul". . . .

From our hearts to your heart . . . Thank you! Thank you! Thank you!

And God Bless You!

ACROPOLIS BOOKS, LTD.
11741 Bowman Green Dr.
Reston, VA 22090

Attention: Schools and Corporations
ACROPOLIS books are available at quantity discounts with bulk purchase for educational, business, or sales promotional use. For information, please write to:
SPECIAL SALES DEPARTMENT, ACROPOLIS BOOKS, LTD., 13950 Park Center Rd., Herndon, VA 22071

Library of Congress Cataloging-in-Publication Data
Pechter, Alese. 1940-
  What's in the deep? : an underwater adventure for children / by Alese and Morton Pechter.
    p. cm.
  Summary: While snorkeling at the beach with their parents, Nelson and Patricia go snorkeling with their older cousin and learn many things about the ocean and its inhabitants and the importance of keeping the oceans clean and healthy.
    ISBN 0-87491-983-5 : $14.95
  1. Marine biology—Juvenile literature.
2. Oceanography—Juvenile literature. [1. Marine biology. 2. Oceanography.] I. Pechter, Morton,   . II Title QH91.16.P43 1989
  574.5'2936—dc19   89-6465
                                                        CIP
                                                         AC

Art Direction, cover design, and book design by Kathleen K. Cunningham
Printed in Singapore

Dedication

To our children, Todd, Jay, Stuart and Madeline, Richard and Robin and our grandchildren, William, Joseph, Patricia, Nelson, Diana and Wyatt, and those daughters and grandchildren to come. . . .

May you always follow your dreams . . . realizing that new worlds can be conquered if you vividly imagine, sincerely believe, ardently desire and enthusiastically act.

If you *WANT TO* strongly enough, you can make it happen.

Introduction

Sylvia Earle, Ph.D.
Chief Scientist, NOAA

This is my kind of fish story—one that invites readers to get acquainted with fish and other sea creatures eye-to-eye, on their own terms. Many people know fish primarily as something to eat, nicely browned with butter and slices of lemon, or pets in a bowl. In this elegantly illustrated book, "What's in the Deep?," the Pechters provide a quite different perspective, an intriguing view of the sea as an accessible place filled with fascinating creatures that are curious about the humans who have splashed down in their midst.

This "inner space adventure" is particularly appealing because of an underlying message that, "You, too, can do this. You, yes, *you*, the one reading these lines, can do what the young explorers in the story have done."

In fact, millions of people worldwide have donned masks and flippers and taken the plunge into that liquid blue realm that dominates the planet. They are rewarded with the delight of discovery that fish have personality, octopuses tend to be shy, moray eels are generally gentle, that snorkeling and diving are fun, and that the ocean is an irresistible, enchanting place when viewed from the inside out.

Only a few people in this century can be astronauts, with a chance to view earth from some distant place in space. But almost anyone can become an "aquanaut" and explore inner space. Space exploration is thrilling, but lonely when compared to experiences awaiting everyone who ventures into the sea. Underwater, one can anticipate encounters with giant rays, translucent jewel-like jellies, ephemeral rainbow creatures, and hauntingly familiar fish—in hauntingly unfamiliar surroundings. But first-hand ocean exploration also causes us to see ourselves in a different way, as a part of, not apart from, the living systems that characterize the planet.

Some, of course, are drawn to the sea by the lure of human history written in countless sunken ships and a "rain" of artifacts that have fallen into the depths during many centuries of sea-going travel. Some venture into the sea in search of tangible treasures such as gold bars and silver doubloons. But everyone can share in the ocean's real treasure—life.

This the authors convey as the real significance of the underwater experiences described and beautifully illustrated in this book. Snorkeling and diving are fun, the creatures in the sea are amusing, appealing, curious, and endlessly fascinating—but more importantly they, and the good health of the oceans generally, are tremendously important to the future of mankind.

As a child, I had the good fortune to live near the sea, first in New Jersey and later in Florida. My parents encouraged my inclination to play in the bay near our Gulf of Mexico home, and gave me my first "window" into the deep, a face mask, when I was about the age of the characters in this story. It took many years of chance encounters with thousands of fishes and crabs and jellyfishes and corals and other sea creatures to slowly learn much of what is conveyed so beautifully here.

How I wish there had been a book like this available then, one that could show me that rays and sharks and morays and critters generally are not dangerous, but rather, that they are fantastic beings, more wonderful than anything conjured up in science fiction yarns. Some who read this book may never go into the sea themselves, and will have only the pleasure of vicariously viewing the sea from the standpoint of those who live there. Others, (and I hope *all*), will someday find themselves gliding freely among the fish into the deep, deep, deep.

Sylvia A. Earle

It was a fine day early in the summer when Nelson and Patricia arrived at the beach with their mom and dad. They met their cousin Todd who was home from college for the summer. He couldn't wait to show them what he'd learned about the ocean.

The sand was bright gold, and white sparkles of sunlight flashed on the tops of the waves. On the beach, Nelson and Patricia looked out at the beautiful blue water.

"What do you think is down in the water, Todd . . . deep, deep down?" Patricia asked.

"All kinds of things," Todd answered. "Lots of plants and animals and little fish and big fish. The ocean is full of life. Would you like to see?"

Nelson turned to his father and asked, "Dad, may we go snorkeling with Todd?"

"Of course you can, if you're careful and stay close to Todd," Dad replied. "I'll help you get ready."

Why don't you pretend you are going snorkeling? First you clear your mask by spitting into it, rubbing it with your fingers, and then rinsing it in the water until it is clear. Then put it on so you can look down into the water without getting water in your eyes. Put the mouthpiece of your snorkel into your mouth. Take a few normal breaths through the snorkel to make sure you are comfortable. Now you're ready to swim away with Patricia and Nelson.

While Mom and Dad went into the equipment locker to get the snorkeling gear, Patricia and Nelson told Todd a secret.

"We want to see a shark," said Patricia.

Nelson nodded. "Don't tell Dad and Mom. Do you think we'll find one, Todd?"

Todd smiled and shrugged his shoulders. "Sharks are very unpredictable," he said. "We might see one, or we might not."

Just then Mom and Dad came back with their arms full of snorkeling equipment, so Patricia and Todd and Nelson waded into the ocean and sat down. On went the fins, on went the masks. Nelson slipped the strap of his waterproof camera around his neck. If there was a shark, he wanted a picture. Who

would believe he'd seen a shark without proof? People talked about sharks, but no one he knew had ever seen a real one.

"Remember the rules," Dad said. "Stay together, and stay close to shore. I'll be right here, watching. If you want me to come out, just raise one arm and wave."

They puffed once through their snorkels to make sure there was no water in them, and then swam off with their faces in the water, their snorkels sticking up like little chimneys. It was easy, like floating in a bathtub, and the snorkels gave them all the fresh air they needed. Now they were ready to see for themselves what was down there in the deep.

Pretend you are floating along the top of the turquoise water with the children, looking way down at all the fish swimming below you.

Taking Underwater Photographs

To take underwater pictures you must use a special camera that is designed to prevent water from entering and damaging it. Several companies make these cameras. In addition, you can put any regular camera into a watertight case and use it to take pictures under water.

Ribbons of sunlight flickered on the uneven sand of the sea bottom. Swarms of tiny tropical fish swam quickly by. As they made their way out from shore, they could see their shadows gliding along the snowy white sand below them.

Closer to shore, on a dock, some scuba divers got ready to dive in. Like Nelson, Todd and Patricia, they wore masks and fins, but they also had tanks filled with air that let them swim under the water for a long time. The scuba divers jumped into the water and swam off.

Patricia spotted something on the bottom. It was gray and shaped like a triangle. Was it a seashell? She held her breath, dove down, and snatched it up. Quickly returning to the surface, Patricia took the snorkel out of her mouth and called to her brother and cousin. They swam over to see what she had found.

"Look at this," Patricia said. The flat object had sharp edges.

"Wow!" Nelson exclaimed. "What is it?"

"That's a fossilized shark's tooth," Todd explained.

Taking pictures while snorkeling requires patience and practice. You must be comfortable with your face mask, snorkel and fins, and with the skills of snorkeling.

There are a few basic pointers to keep in mind when taking underwater pictures.

1. Underwater objects appear much larger and closer than they actually are. What is really 4 feet away appears to be 3 feet away. You should set your camera for the distance it appears to be underwater.

2. Start by taking pictures of subjects that remain in one place, such as corals, sponges and sea fans. They are much easier to photograph than fast swimming fish.

3. Get as close as you can to the subject of your photo. The closer you are, the clearer the picture will be.

4. Take most of your photos between 10 a.m. and 2 p.m. when the sun is high above you. Hold the camera steady, look through the viewfinder, get in as close as you can and start snapping.

That is the key to success—keep at it, be patient, keep practicing. Good luck!

Sea Fans

Shark Teeth In The Sand

You might find a shark's tooth at almost any beach. Shark teeth can be any size, as small as your thumbnail or as big as your fist. Not all sharks have triangular teeth, and those that do, also have slender teeth. Sharks have five rows of teeth. When a tooth falls out, they just grow a new one. Each shark has thousands of teeth in its life. Millions of years ago there was a giant shark called a "megalodon." Each of its teeth was almost as big as your head! You can find megalodon teeth today in the Chesapeake Bay area of coastal Delaware.

"Does that mean there's a shark nearby?" Patricia asked.

"No, sharks lose teeth all the time. That particular one was lost many, many years ago and was probably washed in near shore by the currents. But it's possible that there may be a shark around here someplace. Let's follow the scuba divers. Maybe we'll see a shark with them."

Nelson kept his camera ready as they followed the divers. They all swam over the sand and glided into a field of big boulders. These boulders were bigger than Nelson and Patricia—even bigger than Todd or the di-

Christmas Tree Worms

vers—and they reached up almost to the surface of the water. The boulders were wrinkled, with patches of brilliant color spattered on their surface.

They had found a reef! Sea fans swayed in the currents. Brightly colored small Christmas tree worms sparkled. Hundreds of fish swam in and out looking for food. Nelson had never seen so many fish. He felt as if he were in a huge aquarium.

Patricia thought it looked like an underwater garden. The children motioned to each other, then pulled out their snorkels, as they floated freely on the surface of the water.

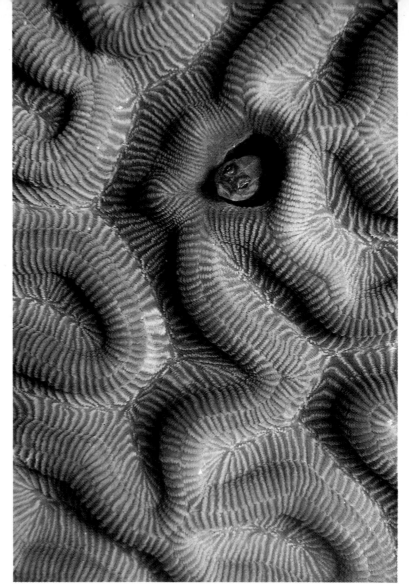

Brain Coral with Goby (close up)

Corals: Animals or Rocks?

Corals look like rocks, but they are really animals. In fact, they are some of the most amazing creatures in all of nature. The coral pictured above is a colony of brain corals. A colony is any group of animals, insects or plants that lives together. An ant hill is a colony. So is a hive full of honey bees.

There are many different kinds of corals. Each different kind of coral is called a "species." Coral colonies always contain corals of the same species. Each species has its own distinctive scientific name and many have common names.

The colony above is called a brain coral because its outside looks like the furrows and ridges on the outside of your brain.

"We've found a coral reef," said Todd. "It looks like a garden, but it's really a colony of animals—coral animals—called *polyps*. Each colony is home to many of these corals, just like an apartment building can be home to many people. During the day, some polyps hide inside their hard coral 'home,' but at night they pop out like flowers and extend

Star Coral Polyps at night (close up)

their arms to catch food. Like so many other creatures in the sea, many corals feed mostly at night."

"Be careful of the corals," he warned. "If you touch one of them, you might accidentally break off a piece and kill it. They look hard on the outside, but they are really very fragile."

Only the very outside layer of the colony is alive. When a coral polyp on the outside of a colony dies, a new polyp settles down on top of the dead polyp's skeleton. Over many years, the coral colony slowly grows in size, as layers of new coral grow on top of the older corals. The inside of the colony is made up of stony skeletons of dead coral polyps.

If you were to cut a coral colony in half, you would see rings that marked these layers, one outside of another, just like the growth rings that show on a tree stump. Like trees, corals grow very slowly.

Even in very warm water, such as the Caribbean Sea, many corals grow less than a quarter of an inch per year!

Basket Sponge

Opposite page:
Purple Tube Sponge with
Red Squirrelfish

They put their snorkels back into their
mouths again and set off. With their faces in
the water, as they floated along above the
magical coral kingdom, sounds seemed very
far away. As they glided along they could
see the colorful sponges, some were so big
they looked like baskets, some were long
purple or yellow tubes. Next to a purple
tube sponge was a bright red squirrelfish
with its big eye and dorsal fin standing
erect. Attached to one coral was a pale white
anemone with a tiny colorful shrimp sitting
among its tentacles.

Queen Angel

Opposite page:
Anemone with Shrimp

Suddenly a beautiful fish appeared from behind a sea fan. It had deep blue scales with golden flecks, and it looked right up at Nelson and Patricia. Much to their surprise, the angelfish swam right up to meet them. The children were charmed. The angelfish watched them for a minute or two, then swam in and out and all around them, as if it had been just waiting for someone to play tag.

With a tiny blue crown on top of its head, this was a Queen angelfish.

The next time they all rested, Patricia declared, "I think this little fish wants to be our friend. I'm going to name it Jamie."

Gray Angel

"I'll bet Jamie has seen a lot of wonderful things," Todd said, "Maybe even a shark."

Patricia looked at the tooth she'd found. "Do you think we'll see a shark?"

"Why do you want to bother with a shark so much?" Todd asked.

"Because we've never seen one, except in books," Nelson said.

"There are many more beautiful fish to look at than sharks," said Todd.

"There is so much food in a coral reef that hundreds of different kinds of fish can live here. You'll see they are all the colors in your paint box, and they come in funny shapes, too."

"Are sharks dangerous?" Patricia asked stubbornly, almost ignoring Todd.

"Well, you can never tell about sharks," Todd said.

"We're not afraid," Nelson said, bravely.

"We want to take a picture of a shark with our underwater camera," Patricia explained.

"All right," Todd grinned, "we'll look for a shark. Follow me." He turned, flicked his fins and went gliding over the reef. Patricia and Nelson followed.

"Look!" Patricia cried to her companions. "Jamie's following us too."

As they watched through their swim masks, Jamie swam up to one of her cousins, the gray angelfish with a straight-edged flat tail. Then another cousin, the French angelfish swam into view, sparkling with a yellow speck on each one of its scales.

French Angel

"Maybe it's called a French angelfish," Patricia thought, "because it looks so fashionable."

Nelson was thinking, "These fish are very pretty. But where are the sharks?"

Todd motioned for the children to follow him. He swam toward the scuba divers on the other side of the reef.

Let's follow the children. Put on your snorkeling gear again and let's go. . . .

How the Parrotfish Got Its Name

Parrotfish are fascinating creatures. Divers and fishermen call them parrotfish because of their parrot-like beaks. Parrotfish have very strong beaks. They need them to eat coral, which is their main food. After coral passes through a parrotfish's stomach, it's turned into sand. Although most parrotfish are only about a foot long, just one of them may produce as much as a ton of sand each year. That's enough sand to fill a dump truck, or enough to fill your backyard to several feet deep!

Parrotfish

The trio swam up and over the reef with Jamie in the lead, hugging the tops of the corals as she went. Patricia and Nelson followed just above her on top of the water. They swam around the other side of the reef, and when they had almost reached the end of the corals, Patricia suddenly pointed excitedly to a parrotfish having its lunch nearby. It had the most beautiful scales, as colorful as any bird's feathers, and a strong beak to scrape the coral with its teeth. The children watched as it chewed and chewed,

Parrotfish

At night, parrotfish spin themselves a transparent cocoon and go to sleep. No one is quite sure what purpose the cocoon serves. Some scientists think it prevents their enemies from detecting them. Scuba divers who swim on reefs at night often see parrotfish floating in a cubbyhole under the coral, each one fast asleep in its own sleeping bag.

leaving crumbs of coral in its wake. Nelson and Patricia swam down to examine its handiwork. The sand all around the bottom of the reef was made up of tiny particles of ground-up coral. It looked like sand, a gleaming carpet of white sand that skirted the reef in all directions. The children were amazed to think of how many years of chewing it had taken to make so much sand.

"He sure has some appetite!" Patricia thought.

Parrotfish spinning a cocoon

Scorpionfish

Trumpetfish

Now imagine you can see into the water, where fish often play "hide and seek." They either change their colors or find a place where they are hard to see. They can even blend in with the corals and the rippling sand and plants. This is called *camouflage*.

If you look closely, you'll see a scorpionfish hiding next to the coral. The spots of color and the leafy growth on its face make the scorpionfish look just like a coral rock covered with algae.

There's a trumpetfish hanging upside down in the clumps of soft coral. When the waves move them around, their bodies bend and sway just like the soft coral branches.

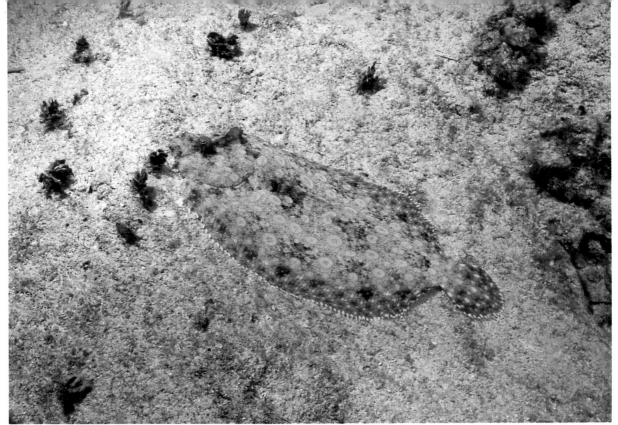
Peacock Flounder

A pair of eyes popped up from under the fresh sand left behind by the parrotfish. They rolled up and back, taking in the curious trio. Their new friend was a peacock flounder. "Those bumps are his eyes," said Todd, as he blew the water out of his snorkel. "The flounder's eyes are both on the same side of his head. He can lie flat on the sand and even though you're getting quite near, you won't see him, no matter how closely you peer."

Patricia and Nelson were impressed by how easily the flounder could hide in the sand. The flounder just shook himself off and swam away to look for a new hiding place.

Another curious fish swam by.

Scrawled Filefish

Right:
Cowfish

Below:
Bright Blue Cowfish

"That's a scrawled filefish," said Todd. "He has black spots and beautiful blue markings on his body. As he swims along he can change his color from very pale to very bright."

"Why does he do that?" Patricia asked.

"He changes his color to blend in with the seascape," answered Todd. "That way he can search for food without being seen by his enemies."

"Do all fish play tricks with their colors?" Patricia asked Todd.

"Most of them do have some way of fooling bigger fish," Todd agreed. "This one here is a cowfish. He's covered by a hard shell. See the two 'horns' on top of his head? The horns make him hard to swallow, so the bigger fish pass him by when they're looking for a meal."

"Would the shark pass him up for something easier to swallow?" Patricia asked.

Trunkfish

"Oh, no," Todd said. "When it comes to getting a meal, sharks aren't put off by anything. They've been known to take a bite out of an old tire or an oil drum."

The next fish they spotted was a white spotted trunkfish. His body was covered with a solid shell just like the cowfish, sort of like a knight's suit of armor, or an old-fashioned steamer trunk. That's why he's called the trunkfish.

Just then two of the divers swam by in a great stream of bubbles. They were chasing one of the strangest things Nelson and Patricia had ever seen. It was round, and had shiny eyes and big spikes all over it.

"What's that?" Nelson shouted, as he yanked out his snorkel in excitement.

"That's a porcupinefish," Todd said. "When he gets frightened, he blows up like a beach ball. His spines make him too much of a mouthful for most fish, but he is probably not sure about the 'bubblefish' who are chasing him. We know those divers won't hurt him. They just want to take his picture while he is blown up that way."

Todd pointed to a Nassau grouper, with black stripes on his face. The Nassau grouper can change colors as easily as we change our clothes. It helps him to blend in with the reef in case some other fish wants to make him his snack.

Todd led Nelson and Patricia to a spot on the outside of the reef where the bottom was very steep. They could see the wreck of an old sailing ship, sitting on the sand below.

Coral grew on its hull. The sails were gone, and its two tall masts lay on the bottom, half covered with sand. It had been underwater a very long time, and there wasn't much of it left. Certainly far less than you would need to sail with on top of the water. The ship still had a purpose, though.

"The ship is a sort of reef, with lots of places for small fish and big fish to hide," Todd said.

Nassau Grouper

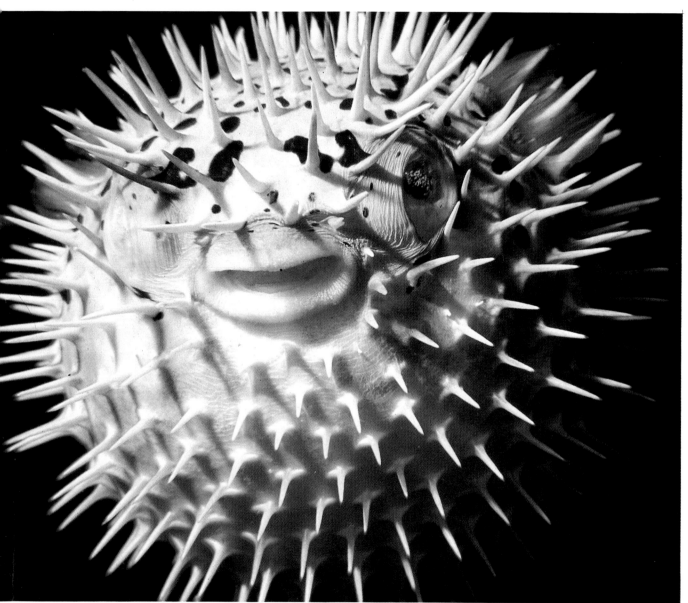

Porcupinefish

Four-eyed Butterfly

Nelson, Patricia and Todd swam around a corner of the ship with the little Queen angelfish, Jamie, still following along.

A school of four-eyed butterflyfish appeared with black spots on their backs that looked like an extra pair of eyes. The children guessed that a big fish would have trouble telling whether it were chasing the butterflyfish's head or its tail. Then the children spotted a Spanish hogfish with bright colors on its side.

Nelson looked down at the ship and wondered what may be hidden inside. "Maybe there's pirate gold down there," Nelson said.

"I doubt it," said Todd, "but there is cer-

Spanish Hogfish

tainly lots of 'treasure' hidden within its old timbers."

"What kind of treasure?" Patricia asked.

"I'll ask you a question and the first letters of the four answers will spell out the name of this 'treasure,' " said Todd. "Are you ready?"

"There is something even more valuable to us than gold. You see, without the ocean, this treasure wouldn't be possible."

"Here's the first question. The ocean covers more than two-thirds of the entire surface of the earth. Without any landmarks to help them find their way, sailors measure their location on the ocean by using numbers called longitude and _____."

With that strange name you must be wondering whether the hogfish is greedy at dinnertime or how else could it have a piggy name like that? Patricia and Nelson wondered, too. If all of you look carefully, you'll see that his short nose and hog snout make him look just like a hog.

Here is a game that Todd played with Nelson and Patricia. See if you know the answers, as you play along with them.

Diving in Submarines

Since water weighs more than air, the deeper you go under the water, the more pressure there is on your body. In fact, the pressure increases by almost 15 pounds per square inch for each 33 feet of depth. Think of how much your mom or dad weighs. Then imagine all of their weight pressing down on just one square inch of your body. That's how hard the water would press on you at a depth of about 300 feet. Divers who work on the platforms that drill for oil in the ocean dive as deep as 600 feet, sometimes deeper.

Below 900 feet, the pressure is too intense even for these trained divers. To go deeper, scientists have invented submarines that can dive more than two miles below the surface.

Incredibly, they found life flourishing in this region where no sunlight ever penetrates and the water pressure could crush the body of an automobile. Giant worms, some of them 12 feet long, live around the edges of cracks where the hot water comes out of the ocean floor.

"I know that one," said Nelson, "My science teacher taught us that. The answer is *latitude*. Latitude is a number that tells us how far you are from the equator."

"Very good," said Todd. "And did you know that the equator is exactly halfway between the North Pole and the South Pole? Sailors call the equator 'zero degrees latitude.' The higher the latitude number, the farther you are from the equator and the closer you are to either the North Pole or the South Pole. The North Pole is at 90 degrees North, while the South Pole is at 90 degrees South."

"Here's the second question. This time I'll put it in a rhyme. 'There's a treasure in the sea that's neither yours nor mine. It's in the salt that's on your table, and we call it_____.'"

"I know that one," called out Patricia. "The answer is *iodine*. Mom told me stories of using iodine as a medicine in the old days. Grandma used to put it on her cuts and scrapes to make them heal faster . . . but it hurt a little. She also told me that there is some iodine in the box of salt we buy at the store."

"That's exactly right, Patricia," said Todd. "Iodine is one of the things that make seawater taste salty. People need a small amount of iodine to stay healthy. That's why it's added to table salt. It is also a very strong medicine. Doctors still use it for some things, but for your cuts and scrapes there are other medicines that will not sting."

Rock Beauty

"Look," said Todd, "There's a beautiful rock beauty. See the black fish with the bright yellow face and tail? See him nibbling at the coral? He's giving you the answer to the next question. There's enough of this treasure in the ocean for every person on the earth to have all they will ever need. Whether it comes from the sea or from land, most people have it three times a day. They call it 'breakfast,' 'lunch,' and 'dinner.'"

"Oh, I know that one," said Patricia. "That has to be food."

"Yes," agreed Todd. "There's a great deal of food in the ocean. Fish can be caught with a net or a fishing pole. Seaweed is a popular food in many parts of the world. Some scientists are even learning how to build fish 'ranches' to raise fish the same way ranchers raise cows on land. Someday, people might have jobs as 'fishboys,' using a submarine to herd fish from one part of the ranch to another."

"Now we are getting close to our treasure," said Todd. "We have the letters 'L,I,F.' We need just one more. Oh, look at that fish over there. That bright red one with the big eyes. They call him 'big-eye,' And the first letter of 'eye' will give you a hint for the next answer.

"Can you tell me the name of a very special planet in our solar system that is different from all the eight other planets in one very special way? They call this place the 'water planet' because it has more wet places than dry places. The water makes the green plants grow, and from outer space it looks like a bright blue ball falling through space."

"That's easy," said Nelson. "That has to be our own planet, the earth."

"Right you are, Nelson," said Todd. "The earth is unique among the nine planets in our solar system because two-thirds of it is covered with water. The sun heats the water in the ocean, turning it into water vapor, which is like the steam that comes out of a tea kettle when you heat it on the stove. The

Big Eye

water vapor forms clouds, which drift over the land where the clouds release their water and it rains. The rains fall to the ground, providing water to drink and water to raise food, like corn, wheat, and green peas. Eventually the water collects in rivers and streams and returns to the ocean. Of course, if the people do not take care of the water, if they put chemicals and trash into it, or kill too many of its animals, it is not very good for us or the fish to swim in."

"Oh, Todd, now we know the answer," called out Nelson and Patricia. "The last letter we needed was 'E.' The real treasure in the ocean is *LIFE*."

"Exactly," said Todd.

The Ocean is Life

Without the ocean, life wouldn't be possible. The sun would make the Earth too warm. There would be no water to make plants grow. Since plants make the oxygen you and I need to breathe, we wouldn't be alive, and there would not be any fish or reef for us to see. So you have found the real treasure of the ocean, it is not gold but "LIFE."

Did you guess all the answers?

Bristleworm

Fire Coral

"Come on, now," Todd called, "Let's go back to the shallower water, but be careful of that little red thing. It's a bristleworm, and it can sting a little. There's some fire coral. It really isn't coral at all; someone just named it that. If you brush against it, it will sting you, but not too badly. It would feel like a mosquito bite."

"Are we ever going to see a shark?" asked Nelson.

"Be patient," Todd said. "Sharks make a point of staying out of sight. Nobody knows why; it's just their way. Sharks puzzle everyone. You can never tell what they'll do

Sea Turtle

next. They are really unpredictable. They go their own way and the rest of us keep a safe distance."

One of the divers swam near, following a shape that was big and dark. It was a turtle. He has a hard shell to protect him from almost all of the fish, no matter how big they are. This has helped him to live to be very, very old. He is probably older than your great grandfather and slow like great grandfather too. Once these turtles lived on land. Later, for some reason, they decided they liked life in the sea much better. When the time comes for a mother turtle to lay her

French Grunts

Grunts and Goat fish

Listen carefully and you'll hear their sound!

eggs, she returns to land and makes her nest on the beach. Soon after, she returns to the ocean. When the baby turtles hatch, they have to find their own way down to the beach and across the sea. No one really knows how they do it.

Patricia and Nelson and Todd swam on, following one of the divers who was exploring a small crack in the reef. As the diver came over the top of a ledge, dozens of blue and gold fish rushed out from under the coral. They were french grunts.

Patricia and Nelson listened, and they heard the fish. It sounded as if they were talking to each other. The fish were making

Blue Spotted Ray

low grunting noises as they moved back and forth over the reef.

Patricia, Nelson, and Todd kept swimming, over the top of a ledge of coral and down the other side. There they found a stingray parked in the sand. He is a cousin to the shark. The sides of his body look like big wings and he moves them up and down to make himself move, as you do with your arms when you play airplane. The stingray may not look like a shark, but they are cousins because neither of them has any bones. Instead of bones, sharks and rays are filled with cartilage.

If you want to know what *cartilage* is, touch your nose. It's kind of stiff. That's because you have cartilage inside to keep it in shape.

Moray Eel

Pirates

Do you believe in pirates? Well, you should.

Pirates aren't just cartoon characters. America, in particular has a long tradition of piracy. Buccaneers, buried treasure, gold doubloons and bloody cutlasses are an important part of our history.

As the three watched, the stingray flapped his great wings and slowly glided off into the blue, sand streaming from his back. Patricia looked back to where she'd first seen the ray, and out of a hole in the coral came a creature that looked like a sea monster. It didn't look like any of the fish they had seen. It was an eel. He may look pretty fierce to you, but that's because he has to keep opening and closing his mouth to pump water over his gills so he can breathe the oxygen that's in the water.

"It's almost time to go back," said Todd. "I hope we get to see your shark soon. Let's go check out what the scuba divers have found."

The divers were looking for a shark, too. Nelson, Todd, Patricia, and Jamie swam far behind the divers. With their cameras, air tanks, and wetsuits, Nelson thought the divers looked as mysterious as a shark.

As they swam through a curtain of bubbles, something in the distance swam right in front of their startled eyes. That something was definitely a shark. He was nosing around the coral, searching for a meal.

The flashlights on the divers' cameras blazed like exploding firecrackers on the Fourth of July. The shark paid no attention. As he swam slowly by the divers, he looked fearless. All the same, it's hard to tell when a shark is afraid. The shark swam slowly around the divers, as if he were inspecting their gear.

The shark is the oldest living thing in the sea. His relatives have been swimming in the ocean for millions of years—longer than people have been walking on the land. We can only hope that sharks will always be around because they help keep the ocean clean. They are sort of like living vacuum cleaners, cleaning up the ocean and eating fish that have died.

Many maritime museums have examples of the goodies the pirates were after.

Blackbeard, Jean LaFitte, Jose Gasparilla and Henry Morgan were all real men. They plundered ships and even attacked fortified cities in North and South America during the Golden Age of Piracy, between 1600 and 1850.

Henry Morgan began his career as a privateer, attacking ships for the English government when it was at war with Spain. So did Blackbeard, whose real name was Edward Teach. But most of these privateers continued to attack ships, kill their crews and steal cargo even during periods of peace.

Shark

Get to Know Your Fins

Scuba divers and fishermen watch out for sharks by looking for their fins. When a shark swims near the surface, its fin often sticks out of the water. Each kind of shark has a different shaped fin. If you know the shape of the fin, you can tell what kind of shark you're looking at.

Not all of the fins you might see sticking out of the water belong to sharks.

Most of the time sharks stay in the deep ocean, but during the day they sometimes come up to the reef to eat, just like the rest of the fish. Sometimes they come alone, and sometimes they come with other sharks. You usually know where other kinds of fish will appear and when, but you can never tell with sharks. They can surprise you!

The shark circled in the distance and appeared to be looking into the coral. Jamie the angelfish sensed danger and made a quick dash into a small crack of the coral.

"Uh oh!" Nelson cried. "Jamie is afraid

Dolphins have triangular-shaped fins which look very much like a shark fin.

Dolphins are the shark's only natural enemy in the ocean. Gangs of bottlenose dolphins, like those that perform in acrobatic shows at oceanariums, sometimes ram a shark one after the other. Since dolphins can swim very fast, the impact of their short, stout noses slamming into the shark is enough to drive it away or even kill it.

she'll be the shark's next meal."

Todd, Patricia and Nelson strained to see the shark as he circled in the distance, its big dorsal fin sometimes cutting the surface above.

"Jamie doesn't mean you any harm," Patricia squeaked to William. She had decided to call the shark William.

"I suppose she doesn't," Todd chuckled. "Even if she did, Jamie is no match for a shark. It's all right, though. Jamie knows to stay inside the coral till the shark, I mean William, moves on."

The shark turned around and headed out to sea. The divers chased after him.

"Look how popular he is," Todd said. "People are fascinated by sharks. That's because they really are the lords of the sea."

Just then, the shark flicked his tail and slowly cruised off into the thick blue haze below. As the shark moved out, Nelson tried to take a picture with his underwater camera, but the shark was disappearing from view. The shark swung his head from side to side, looking towards the group. Nelson thought he looked as though he were grinning.

You had better come back with us, too. We'll swim straight back over the coral reef, over the sponges, back over the stingray who has found himself a new patch of sand to hide in, and back over the parrotfish, who looks up at us from a coral he is chewing for dessert.

Jamie peeked out from her hiding place in the coral and when she saw the shark had gone, she came out to play again.

"It's funny," said Todd, "We know so much about the moon and so little about the bottom of the ocean; but now people are studying it all the time to find out more of its secrets."

Todd called to Nelson and Patricia, "Come on, it's time to go back. We've seen what we came to see and a lot more."

How about you? Will you come snorkeling with us again some time?

Back on the beach, Todd explained, "the health of Jamie and of the ocean and all the fish life in it depends on all of us. Sometimes we put poison in the water without even realizing it. We cut down trees on land. The dirt that once was held fast by the tree roots runs into the ocean and buries the coral, killing the animals.

"We accidentally let oil spill from ships or from oil wells under sea. This oil covers the feathers of seabirds, preventing them from flying, and catching their food. It poisons other ocean creatures. We throw away plastic bags or let our balloons fly away over the ocean. Sea creatures think they are food, try to swallow them and choke. Factories sometimes let poisonous chemicals run into the ocean. All of these things can cause corals and fish to die. They can destroy the greatest treasure of the sea . . . its life. When life in the sea dies, the ocean dies. Without the ocean we cannot live. The earth is the 'water planet' and we all have to work to help keep the ocean healthy and that will help keep people healthy, too."

Nelson and Patricia ran up the beach to their parents, both talking at once. "You wouldn't believe what we saw," they said. "Can we go back to the reef again tomorrow, and will you go with us next time?"

"Of course we will," Mom and Dad agreed.